Adopted by an Owl
The True Story of Jackson the Owl

By Robbyn Smith van Frankenhuyzen

Illustrated by Gijsbert van Frankenhuyzen

Sleeping Bear Press

· ·

In memory of my Father, André,
who encouraged me to make my hobby my career.
He said it would be a road to a fulfilling life. He was right.

Gijsbert

———

For Mom, from all of your daughters.
Your strength is our inspiration. We love you.

Karen, Susan, Robbyn, Sandy, Terry, and Nickie

· ·

Sleeping Bear Press
310 North Main Street
P.O. Box 20
Chelsea, MI 48118
www.sleepingbearpress.com

Printed and bound in Canada.

10 9 8 7 6 5 4 3 2 1

Library of Congress Cataloging-in-Publication Data on file.
ISBN: 1-58536-070-8

———

From the Author

For 20 years we have rehabilitated a wide variety of wild critters, from fawns, foxes, skunks, and crows to opossums, raccoons, rabbits, and owls. Some of the animals were injured adults, others were orphaned babies, but all of them were in need of a little help to get them back into the wild.

Growing up on a farm, as well as my training as an animal technician, prepared me for many of the medical situations that arose. Gijsbert took every opportunity to sketch, paint, and photograph our temporary guests during their stay on the farm. More importantly, Gijsbert was issued all the federal and state permits needed to care for birds of prey. Without these permits, we would never have been able to care for hawks and owls. For good reason, caring for these birds is very tightly regulated and closely monitored. Taking an owl from its nest is dangerous and illegal.

We have cared for many great horned owls but none of them were like Jackson, the owl in this story. His personality was unique from the very beginning and we know that we were lucky to have shared such a close bond with this wild bird. This is the true story of his life with us. Enjoy.

Kathryn Smith van Frankenhuyzen

Thump-thump,
thump-thump…

Nick's eyes popped open. Just moments ago he was pleasantly drifting off to sleep, but a sound, like someone walking across the rooftop, woke him and now he lies silent and alert. Listening…waiting.

Then came a familiar *hoot-hoot-hoo-hoooo,*
hoot-hoot-hoo-hoooo.

Could it be that his friend had come back?

It all began years ago when a young boy
stole a great horned owl chick from its nest.

Bundled against the cold March wind,
the boy retraced his steps into the woods.
For over a week he had secretly watched the
great horned owl parents feed their young.
But as he stared up the giant tree, he began
to have doubts about robbing the nest.
The nest was higher than he remembered.

Taking a deep breath, he took one last look
to make sure the parents were no where
near, then tucked a burlap bag into his belt
and began shimmying up the tree.

Woodland creatures watched in silence as
the intruder grabbed the frightened owlet
from the safety of its nest and stuffed it into
the bag. Its frightened screech pierced the
air, warning the nearby parents of danger.

The boy clung tighter to the tree as the return-
ing parents swooped close to his head. Twice
he nearly dropped the captured owl. As the
protective parents continued their daring attacks,
the boy began his long climb down the tree.
The moment his feet hit solid ground, the boy
raced for home, dodging the endless attacks
of the furious birds.

In the secrecy of his bedroom the boy emptied
the bag onto his bed. The frightened owlet
clacked and hissed at the stranger. Without a
single care for the well-being of the young owl,
the selfish boy smiled and thought to himself,
"Now this is a pet no one else has."

As the owl grew, so did its appetite and the boy
quickly discovered that wild animals were never
intended to be pets. Having an owl wasn't fun,
it was work. It wasn't long before he realized he
didn't even *want* the owl anymore.

Soon after, Nick, with his special license to care for owls, came to take the young bird to a new home.

The car ride was a novel experience. Balanced on the headrest of the passenger's seat, the curious owl stared out the window.

As the car pulled into the driveway, the kitchen door flew open and out ran two young girls. "Where is he? Where is he?" they both squealed. They huddled around the new arrival eagerly discussing a proper name for the bird. Faster than you could say *bouncing, bobbing ponytails* four times, the dimpled girls smiled and announced, "His name is Jackson."

As if on cue, Jackson hooted his approval.

Jackson was too young and inexperienced to live on his own. Until he was ready to be set free, a large cage would be his home. Nick was amazed at how easily the young owl accepted his new family.

They spent many months together becoming friends, but the time finally came when Jackson was ready to go. After saying his good-byes, Nick opened the door and the owl flew confidently into the night.

Jackson was on his own.

Days later, as Nick walked the winding
paths of his farm, he spotted Jackson
following him like a silent shadow
from above. It seemed Jackson
had decided to stay on.

From then on Jackson became a permanent part of the family. He accompanied Nick on every walk, greeted him when he returned home from trips and if he was hungry, he reminded Nick it was time to eat. They became best buddies.

During the cold winter nights, the owl began offering Nick mice that he proudly caught himself. At first, Jackson hooted and waited patiently on the balcony railing for his friend to come out. Nick accepted the gift with thanks, offering it back to the owl the next morning.

But as time passed, Jackson's trust for the family grew stronger. One evening there came a *tap-tap-tap* on the glass door. Confused and sleepy-eyed, Nick opened the door. There standing at the entrance was Jackson holding a mouse in his beak. With a little coaxing, he walked into the room and dropped the mouse into Nick's open hand. His long talons made a sharp *click... click...click* sound as he waddled across the wooden floor and back out the door.

Jackson didn't always bring mice…
and the family wasn't always pleased with his gift.

He was curious about the chickens
and pigeons living on the farm and
often flew into their coops.

The birds did not enjoy Jackson's visits.

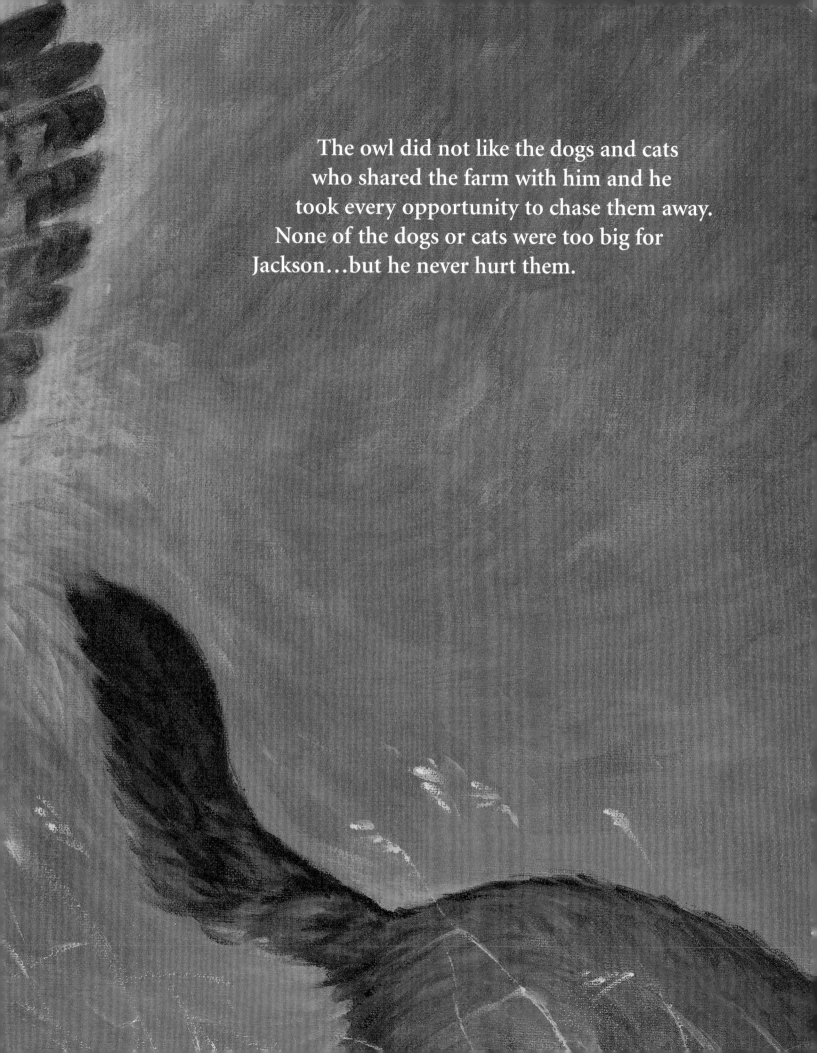

The owl did not like the dogs and cats
who shared the farm with him and he
took every opportunity to chase them away.
None of the dogs or cats were too big for
Jackson…but he never hurt them.

Every morning as the first rays of sunlight filtered through the pine needles, Jackson woke his friend with a *hoot-hoot-hoo-hoo* from his special tree next to the house and Nick hooted back.

They often talked to each other this way.

Sometimes he enjoyed getting wet in the rain.
It was like a refreshing shower cleaning his feathers.

But other times he preferred to stay dry.

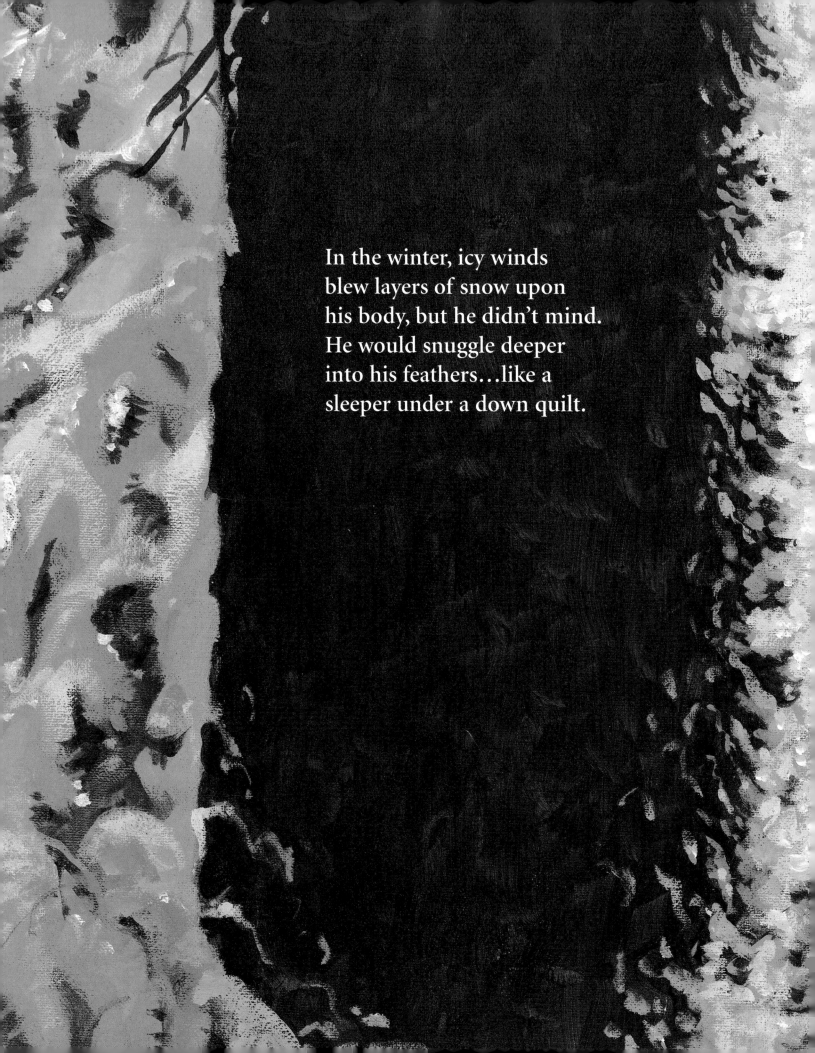

In the winter, icy winds
blew layers of snow upon
his body, but he didn't mind.
He would snuggle deeper
into his feathers…like a
sleeper under a down quilt.

Mother Nature gave him
earth colors in patterns of browns
and grays for camouflage. He tucked his
body tightly against the tree trunk and
used his bark-colored feathers to stay hidden.

But in the springtime, no matter how hard
Jackson tried to hide, birds still found him.

Busy songbirds building nests and raising families did not like him. Bluejays, cardinals, robins and even the tiniest chickadees fearlessly attacked the big owl. The brave little birds swooped angrily around Jackson, plucking feathers from his head to make him go away.

Crows were the only birds able to chase
Jackson from his tree. They pestered
him until he flew away.

A lone blue spruce just at the edge of the meadow was a safe haven for him. He burrowed deep into the branches, safe from the bullying crows.

And if Nick happened to pass below, Jackson
would hoot at him. Soft enough so that the crows
could not hear but loud enough to say to him,
"Hello friend, I am here, safe and sound."

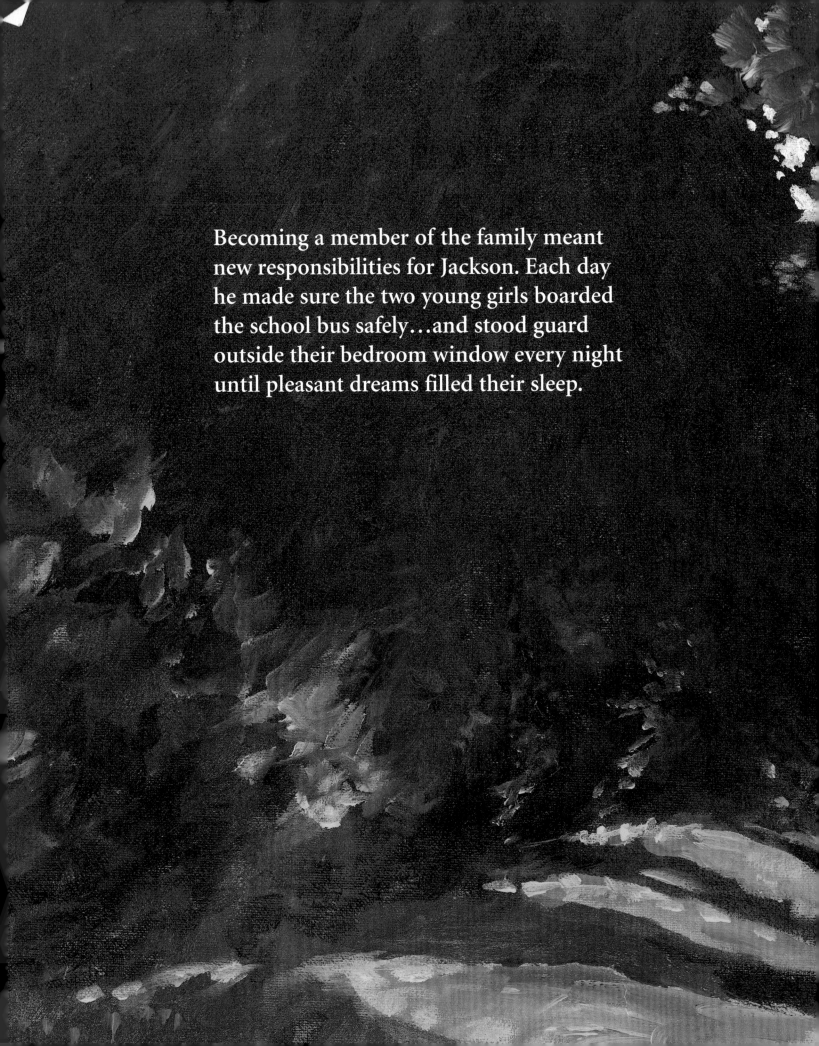

Becoming a member of the family meant new responsibilities for Jackson. Each day he made sure the two young girls boarded the school bus safely…and stood guard outside their bedroom window every night until pleasant dreams filled their sleep.

Then one spring day, Jackson was missing and Nick had a terrible feeling something might be wrong. He searched all of the owl's favorite hiding places and finally found him under the blue spruce.

Trying to stay calm, Nick spoke softly to Jackson. "Shhhh, everything will be all right. I am here now." At the sound of his friend's soothing voice, the injured owl let out a whisper of a hoot. It was all he had left for Nick. Then Jackson collapsed.

Nick rushed the frail bird to a special hospital that cares for injured owls. The doctor took an x-ray of Jackson's leg and showed it to Nick.

"We'll never really know for sure" he said, "but I think your owl was probably hit by a car." The doctor put a large cast on Jackson's broken leg and gave him special medicines that would help the leg heal faster.

While in the hospital, Jackson refused to eat from anyone but Nick, so it became his daily ritual to visit the recovering owl at ten o'clock every morning. "I'm here, my friend," announced Nick. An excited hoot could be heard coming from the long cage-lined wall. In typical owl fashion, Jackson bobbed his head up and down and all around to greet his best friend. It was as if he were announcing, "Finally, I'd thought you'd never get here!"

For months, these visits kept Jackson from becoming frightened or lonely.

At last the day came when the cast was removed and Jackson could go home. Nick helped the owl do special exercises every day to make his leg strong, hoping Jackson would soon be able to fly free again.

Nick kept Jackson in a cage outside his home while he was mending. At night, Jackson began talking to other owls. Many nights, two or three wild owls would talk to him long into the early morning hours. Perhaps it was his stay at the hospital in the company of other injured owls that helped him realize who he really was.

It saddened Nick to think his special friend might leave, but he knew in his heart that the choice must be Jackson's. He loved the large bird and wanted what was best for him.

Finally after a long time, Nick felt Jackson was ready to be set free. He opened the cage door and with Jackson perched on his arm said, "The time has come to stretch your wings and fly proudly." Everyone held their breath. Would he remember his old neighborhood?

The owl took flight, soaring gracefully over the farm. The family smiled with relief as they watched him fly again.

Just then a hoot from the nearby woods called to Jackson and without a single look back, he was gone.

From the very beginning, Nick knew this time would come.
He remembered the car ride home many years ago when
the young owl perched so confidently on the seat. He
knew even then that Jackson was a very special bird.

After Jackson left, Nick spent many
quiet evenings sitting on the balcony.
He smiled as he remembered all the
special times he shared with the
owl and was a little sad that
those times were over.

Then, one night just as the family began
drifting into their dreams, Nick awoke to a
thump-thump, *thump-thump*, like someone
walking across the rooftop and heard a familiar
hoot. As he stepped out onto the balcony,
Jackson swooped low and landed in his
favorite tree next to the house.

Jackson had heard the call of the wild and his
natural instinct was to be with other owls like him.
But he had spent too many years living with his
human family and the pull to come back was too
strong. They both knew he was home for good.

For the rest of his life, Jackson lived on the farm,
flying free and proud, forever watching over his family.

Gijsbert (*Nick*) van Frankenhuyzen

When Gijsbert moved from the Netherlands to America in 1976 no one could pronounce his name, so he was asked to come up with a nickname. "Okay, how about Nick?" he joked, and it stuck. Now he is often called "Mr. Nick" by the thousands of school children he has met while presenting drawing programs in their schools throughout the Great Lakes Region.

Encouraged by his father to make his hobby his career, Nick graduated in Graphic Arts from the Royal Academy of Arts in Arnhem, the Netherlands. He shares his father's message with children of all ages.

Animals have always been one of Nick's favorite subjects to paint. The animals that share the farm with him and his family make excellent models…though not always the most cooperative!

Robbyn Smith van Frankenhuyzen

Robbyn has cared for animals as far back as she can remember, always bringing something injured or orphaned home. She graduated from Michigan State University and worked as an animal technician for many years.

Nick met Robbyn at the animal clinic where she worked, and their common interests in animals made them lifelong friends and partners. Her proudest accomplishment is raising Heather and Kelly, their two wonderfully independent and responsible daughters.

Robbyn kept a journal of Jackson's exceptional life with their family and drew upon those entries to write *Adopted by an Owl*.